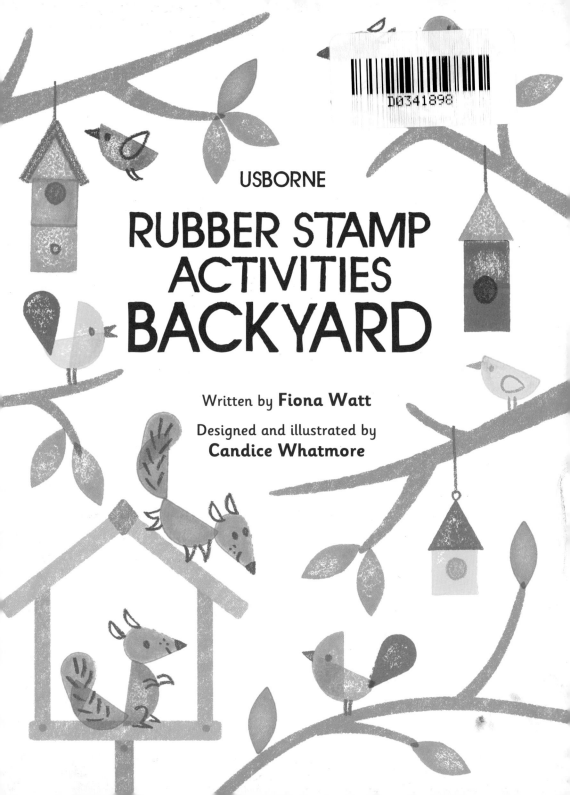

USBORNE

RUBBER STAMP
ACTIVITIES
BACKYARD

Written by **Fiona Watt**

Designed and illustrated by
Candice Whatmore

RUBBER STAMPING TIPS

Press a rubber stamp onto one of the ink pads before printing it on a page in the book.

You can print a shape more than once before pressing onto the pad again, but the prints will get gradually paler.

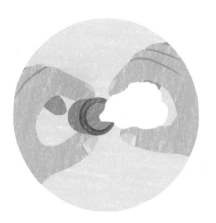

Clean the stamp with a paper towel when you want to use a different ink. When you've finished printing, wash your hands with soap and water to get rid of any ink stains.

Try not to get the inks on your clothes or on a work surface as the inks may stain them.

Wait for the prints to dry completely before drawing on them with a felt-tip pen or adding another stamp on top.

Print lots of apples
and leaves on the tree.

Add lots of spikes to the hedgehogs.

1.

2.

3.

Print more spiders lurking in the shed.

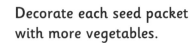

Decorate each seed packet
with more vegetables.

RADISH
SEEDS

Turnip seeds

ONION SEEDS

FINEST QUALITY

SPINACH
seeds

Garden Blooms
PANSY SEEDS

SUNFLOWER

Add more petals to the sunflower.

SEEDS

MARIGOLD
Seeds

Perfect for pots and borders

Decorate these packets with more flowers.

Print seedlings growing
in all the pots.

1.

2.

3.

Bird
SEED
for garden birds

Greenfingers
ORGANIC
PLANT
SPRAY

Add little mice hiding
on the shelves.

1.   2.   3.

GARDEN
TWINE

Print frogs among the stones in the garden rockery.

1.   2.   3.   4.

1.

2.

3.

Add flying bugs around
this hungry toad.

Cover the toad's body
with bumps and lumps.

Stamp bright shells on
the hungry snails.

2.

1.

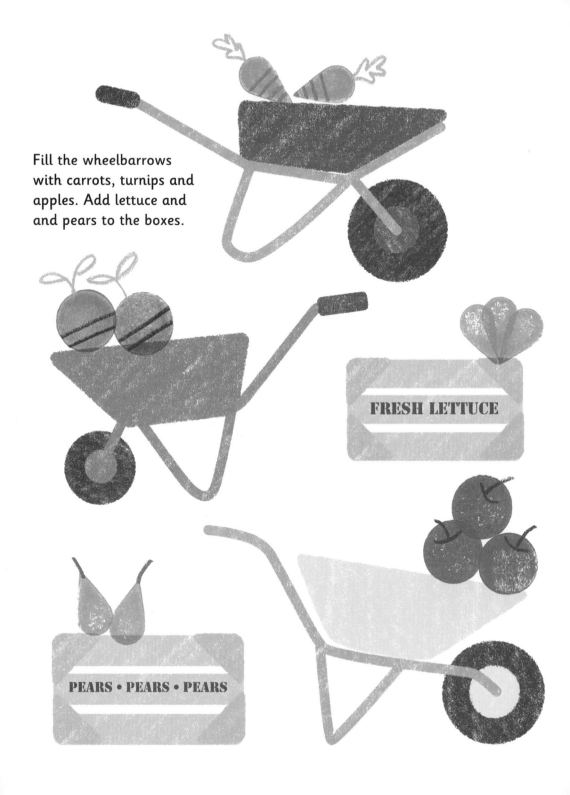

Fill the wheelbarrows with carrots, turnips and apples. Add lettuce and and pears to the boxes.

FRESH LETTUCE

PEARS • PEARS • PEARS

Fill the page with lots of bees.

1.   2.   3.   4.

Add flowers to the
lavender stalks for
the bees to feed on.

You could print
some bees perching
on the lavender.

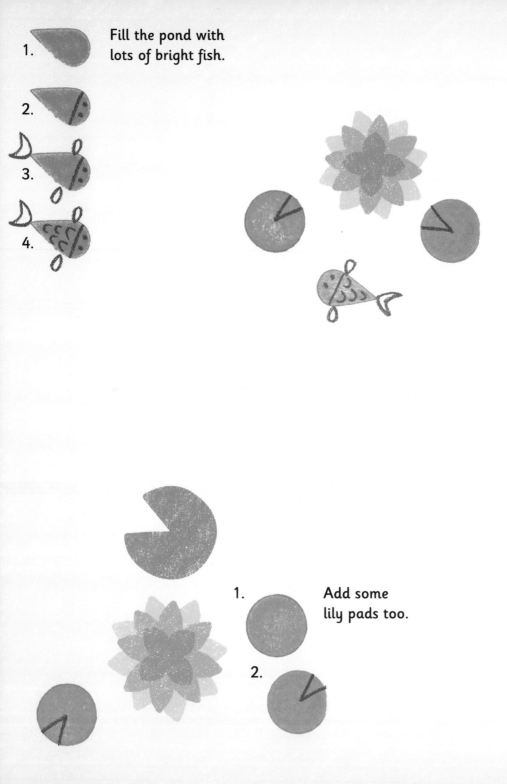

1.

Fill the pond with
lots of bright fish.

2.

3.

4.

1.

2.

Add some
lily pads too.

Print more bird houses hanging from the branches.

Add leaves too.

1.   2.   3.   4.

Fill the page with birds flying or sitting on the branches.

1.   2.   3.

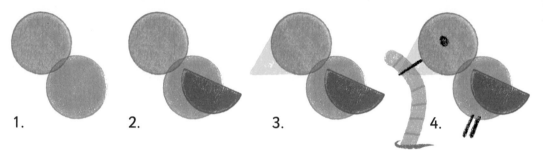

1.

2.

3.

4.

Add more birds pulling up the worms.

Print owls perching
in the trees.

1.

2.

3.

4.

This plant is infested with aphids.

1.

2.

3.

1.

2. Print moles popping out of the molehills.

3.

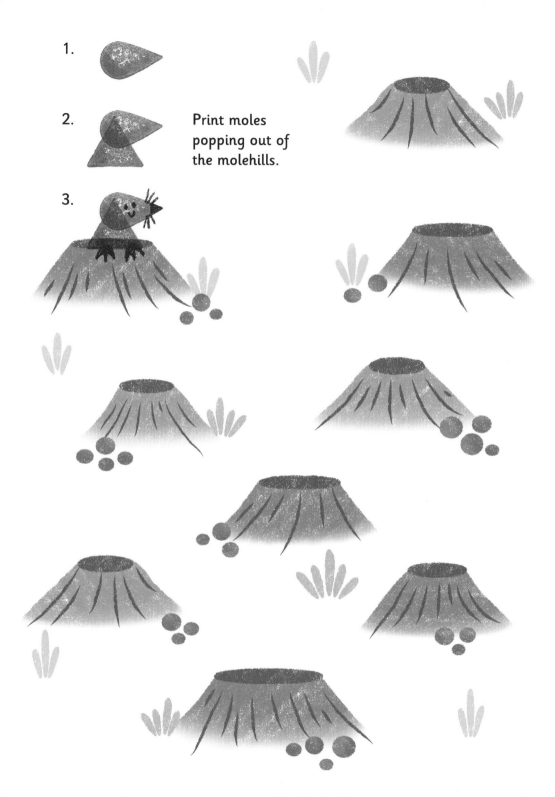

1.

2.

3.

4.

Add hats, beards and faces to the garden gnomes.

Print toadstools too.

Use the half-circle stamp for a wheelbarrow.

Add greedy squirrels
climbing up the bird tables
and on the feeders.

1.　　　　2.　　　　3.　　　　4.

5.

6.

7.

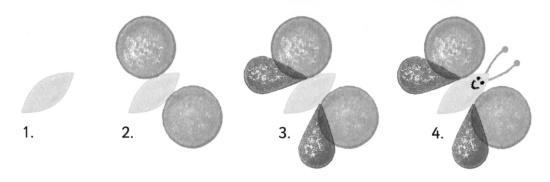

1.　　　2.　　　3.　　　4.

Print butterflies fluttering above the flowers.

Add more petals
to the stalks.

Some butterflies
could have landed
on the flowers.

Print lots of bugs.
Design your own or use
the ideas shown here.

Fill the garden pots with flowers.

Add feathers to
the chickens in
the chicken run.

Print some chicks too.

1. 2. 3. 4.

Print lots of crawling caterpillars. Make them as long or as short as you like.

Add leaves to the bushes.

Stamp patterns all over
the gardening boots.

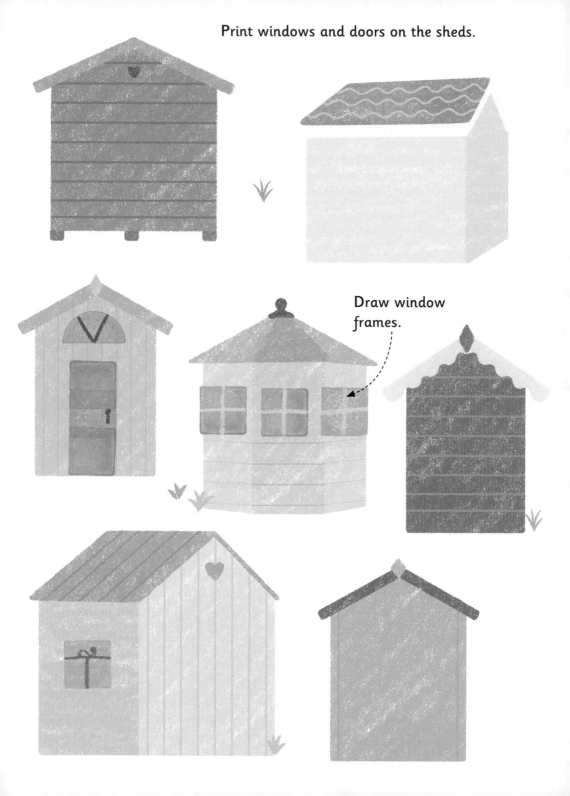

Print windows and doors on the sheds.

Draw window frames.

Print a family of foxes playing in the dark.

1.

2.

3.

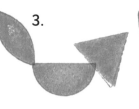

4.

Print a sitting
fox like this.

Add flags to the strings
for a garden party.

Print lots of orange
and lemon slices.

1. 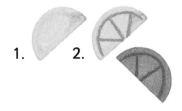 2.

Print lots of red
bugs with spots.

1.

2.

3.

Decorate the flower pots
with different patterns.

Cover the wall with climbing roses and leaves.

1.

2.

Draw the stems after printing the flowers.

Print a feast of acorns for the squirrel.
Add fur on its tail, too.

1.

2.

3.

Print patterns on
the watering cans.

Add petals and leaves
to the sunflowers.

1.

2.

3.

4.

Stamp lots of
birds in the trees.

Add more
nests.

Print ears on the rabbits playing
in the vegetable patch.

Add turnips
poking out of
the ground.

1.

2.

Fill the raised beds with lettuce and tulips.

1. 2. 3.

Add juicy red tomatoes and
green leaves to the tomato plant.

Add big flowers...

1.

2.

ALLIUMS
HALF PRICE

...and lots of leaves.

BOX TOPIARY
2 FOR 1

Print more petals...

LILIES
25% OFF

...and oranges.

Print windows on the houses,
then draw the frames.

Fill the
gardens with
lots of trees.

Add more wasps attracted by the sweet-smelling juice.

1.

2.

3.

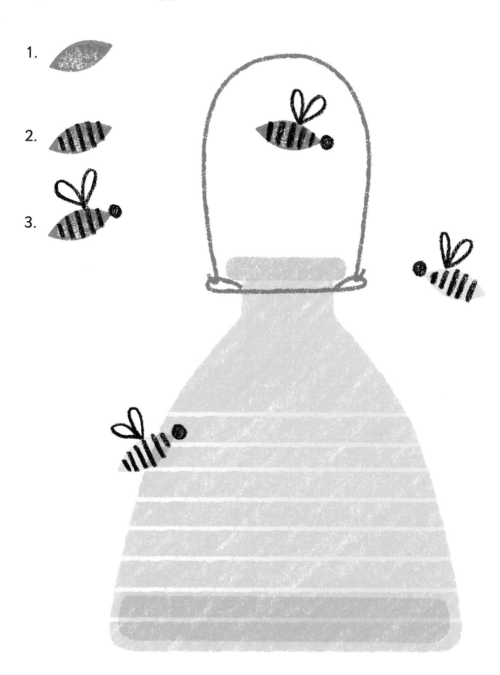

Fill the hanging basket with lots of flowers.

1.

2.

3.

Print flowers
tumbling
out of the
basket, too.

1.

2.

3.

1.   **2.**  **3.**  **4.**

Fill the pages with dogs playing.

Use the half-circle stamp
for a dog lying down.

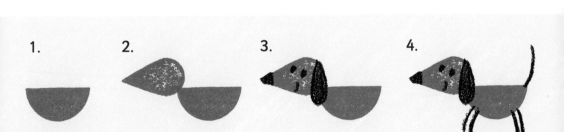

1.   2.   3.   4.

Add cats sitting in the trees and climbing along the fence.

1.

2.

3.

4.

Add some leaves to the trees too.

1.

2.

3.

4.

Print prickly hedgehogs and
lots of leaves for them to
hide between.